Daytona 2009

SILENT NIGHT

by Vicki Howie
illustrated by
Krisztina Kállai Nagy

With Love,
Papa Jerold & Grma Ruth

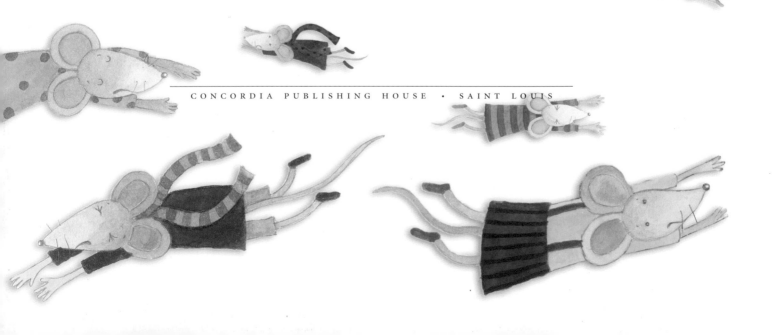

CONCORDIA PUBLISHING HOUSE · SAINT LOUIS

Long ago,
inside a dusty hole,
hidden in the Church of Saint Nicholas
that stood in the village of Oberndorf,
beside a river that rushed helter-skelter
through Austria, a land of music
and mountains and snow,
there lived a large family of mice.

The church mice were very badly behaved.
Whenever the church was quiet, they ran in and out and all around. They chased one another up and down the pulpit and the pews. They swung on the bell ropes and frayed the ends.

Worst of all, they nibbled here and nibbled there until there were holes in books and boards, kneelers and choir robes EVERYWHERE!

But whenever Franz Gruber, the organist and choirmaster, played his rousing music on the church organ, the mice went scampering back to their mouse holes, shaking with fright. Organ music sounds like thunder to a tiny mouse.

One winter afternoon, the mice were startled back to their holes by Franz and kind Father Joseph Mohr who came to church to set out the hymnbooks.

"Are you pleased with the choir, Franz?" asked Father Joseph.

"Certainly," Franz replied. "The music is difficult, but the children sing their parts magnificently!"

"Then I can't wait to hear them tonight at our special Christmas Eve service!" exclaimed Father Joseph. "Their singing is always a highlight of Christmas."

The mice in their mouse holes couldn't know, of course, that it was Christmas Eve. But the people knew! There was the Christmas tree. There was the Christmas crèche. And there was the Christmas Eve worship service.

Soon Franz would shake the rafters with his thunderous chords. That organ would give them such a fright that all the mice would be silent that night!

Again the church mice came out of their holes and again they were startled! This time they were frightened by the sound of the choir children laughing and singing as they made their way to church.

The mice had to get away! But what could they do?
Mice can only scamper and nibble
and scurry and chew, unless . . .
unless they nibbled a hole in the organ bellows.
That would fix things!

Nose to tail, the mice raced toward the bothersome organ. Some ran all over the keys. Others found their way to the bellows.

"Look, Franz! Mice!" cried Father Joseph.

"Oh, no! Not those little rascals again!" muttered Franz. "Just wait until I catch them!"

The mice began to nibble furiously. *Nibble, nibble.*

They hurried to chew the leather bellows to make a hole and get away. They perked up their ears. Footsteps were coming close. *Nibble, nibble.*

Franz and Father Joseph came closer.
Surely those mice would be caught!
Nibble, nibble, and chew!
Finally they were through.

A hole at last! Those naughty mice ran for their lives!

"Take your places quickly, please, children!" said Franz, as the last mouse scurried away. "It's time to practice!"

The choir stood in line and waited for Franz to play the introductory music . . .

But what was this? The organ muttered and sputtered. It gave a cough and a wheeze. Then nothing. The naughty church mice had silenced the organ!

Franz and the children were sad. There would be no organ music that night.

"What shall we do now that the organ's broken?" asked a choirboy, almost in tears. "We can't sing our parts without the help of the organ."

"I'm so sorry!" sighed Father Joseph. "All your hard work is wasted. But here: let's sing a song together to cheer ourselves up."

Father Joseph strummed a few chords on his old guitar. It made such a charming sound that they all felt better.

"Father Joseph, why don't you write us a song for the service tonight?" asked a choir girl.
"You could accompany us on your guitar!"
But Father Joseph only shook his head.

"What would everyone think of a simple guitar at
the Christmas Eve service instead of the organ?" he said.
"No, we will just have to do without your beautiful singing."
The mice peeked out of their mouse holes as the
disappointed people left the church to trudge back home. And
this time, no happy song floated on the cold night air.

The church was quiet again, but it wasn't empty. There was Mary, the young mother, gazing at baby Jesus as He slept peacefully in the animal's manger. There was Joseph, who had taken good care of Mary and baby Jesus.

There were the angels who had streamed from heaven singing, "Alleluia! Christ the Savior is born!"

And there were the shepherds who had trembled at the sight and then hurried to kneel before the Son of God, who came into the world as a tiny baby.

Last there was baby Jesus Himself, who came to love and forgive and save everyone!

There was Father Joseph, too, who suddenly remembered a piece of paper in his pocket. He took it out and began to read a poem written in his own handwriting.

"Stille Nacht, heilige Nacht! . . ."
It sounded like the words of a lullaby for the
baby Jesus.

"I wonder . . ." Father Joseph said aloud.
"I wonder. . . ."

Then, with a nod of his head, he wrapped his
cloak around himself and set out for Franz Gruber's
home in the nearby village of Arnsdorf.

Franz and his family were surprised to have a visitor on Christmas Eve. Father Joseph explained why he had come.

"Dear friend," he said, "I need your help. Could you write a simple tune on the guitar for my Christmas poem? We could sing it tonight, and the choir could join in with the chorus."

"Come on in!" said Franz. "Please, join us for some supper, and I'll see what I can do!"

Clang, clang!
The church bell rang, inviting the
villagers to the Christmas Eve service.

Soon every row was filled with families, all expecting
to hear magnificent organ music.

The people listened as Father Joseph explained that
something had gone wrong with the organ that afternoon.

"I didn't know what to do," he said. "But as I looked at
our crèche, I remembered that Jesus, the Son of God,
was born in a humble stable.

"He is happy with simple things, kindly given. And so
Franz and I have written a simple carol. It's called
'Silent Night' and it is our gift to you."

Father Joseph strummed the opening chords
and the two men began to sing:

> *Silent Night, holy night!*
> *All is calm, all is bright*
> *Round yon virgin mother and child.*
> *Holy Infant, so tender and mild,*
> *Sleep in heavenly peace,*
> *Sleep in heavenly peace.*

Then happy boys and girls joined the chorus.

And the congregation was
so delighted with the new carol
that they didn't notice
a large family of mice
sleeping peacefully
under the Christmas tree.

Silent night, holy night!
　　All is calm, all is bright
Round yon virgin mother and child.
Holy Infant, so tender and mild,
　　Sleep in heavenly peace,
　　Sleep in heavenly peace.

Silent night, holy night!
　　Shepherds quake at the sight;
Glories stream from heaven afar,
Heav'nly hosts sing, Alleluia!
　　Christ, the Savior, is born!
　　Christ, the Savior, is born!

Silent night, holy night!
　　Son of God, love's pure light
Radiant beams from Thy holy face
With the dawn of redeeming grace,
　　Jesus, Lord at Thy birth,
　　Jesus, Lord at Thy birth.